Disney · PIXAR

Let Your Dreams Soar

PIXAR1256473

Code is valid for your Disney·Pixar ebook and
may be redeemed through the Disney Story Central app
on the App Store. Content subject to availability.
Parent permission required.
Code expires on December 31, 2019.

Bath · New York · Cologne · Melbourne · Delhi
Hong Kong · Shenzhen · Singapore · Amsterdam

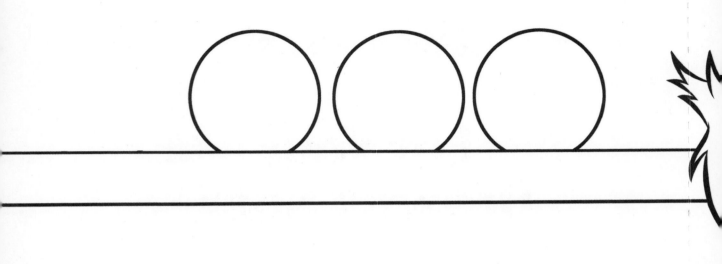

Riley is an awesome hockey player!

© Disney/Pixar

Meet the Emotions—Joy, Sadness, Fear, Anger, and Disgust!

Anger, Fear, and Disgust are lost without Joy and Sadness.

Bing Bong is Riley's imaginary friend!

Long Term Memory is a huge maze!

Andy brings more toys for Bonnie!

Ooh! The Aliens have spotted The Claw!

Muddy Hamm gets a bath.

Jessie and Bullseye make a great team!

"To infinity and beyond!"

Rex has some roar-some, new, dino buddies!

Lotso is in charge of the toys at Sunnyside Daycare.

Spanish Buzz loves to dance!

"Wheee!" Woody is flying high!

Good night, sleep tight.

Ta-da! Mike found Boo's missing bedroom door.

Randall picks his next door.

Sulley has found a small surprise—he names her Boo.

Look at all the little monsters!

Contamination alert! Call the Child Detection Agency!

Randall is a very scary monster.

Sulley and Mike are the top scare team at Monsters, Inc.

Mr. Ray knows lots of cool stuff!

© Disney/Pixar

Crush and Squirt ride the East Australian Current.

Dory thinks the jellyfish are so pretty!

Nigel tells Nemo that his father is on the way.

Whoooo! Wheeeee! Dory speaks whale!

Don't worry, fish are friends!

Which way? This way!

Nemo is excited for his first day of school.

Joy likes group hugs!

Riley has a lot of fun with her mom and dad.

Joy and Sadness make a great team!

Meet Arlo the Apatosaurus.

Who is this little critter?

Glowing fireflies are so pretty!

© Disney/Pixar

Arlo names the critter Spot.

The T. rexes aren't as scary as they look!

A game of hide-and-seek!

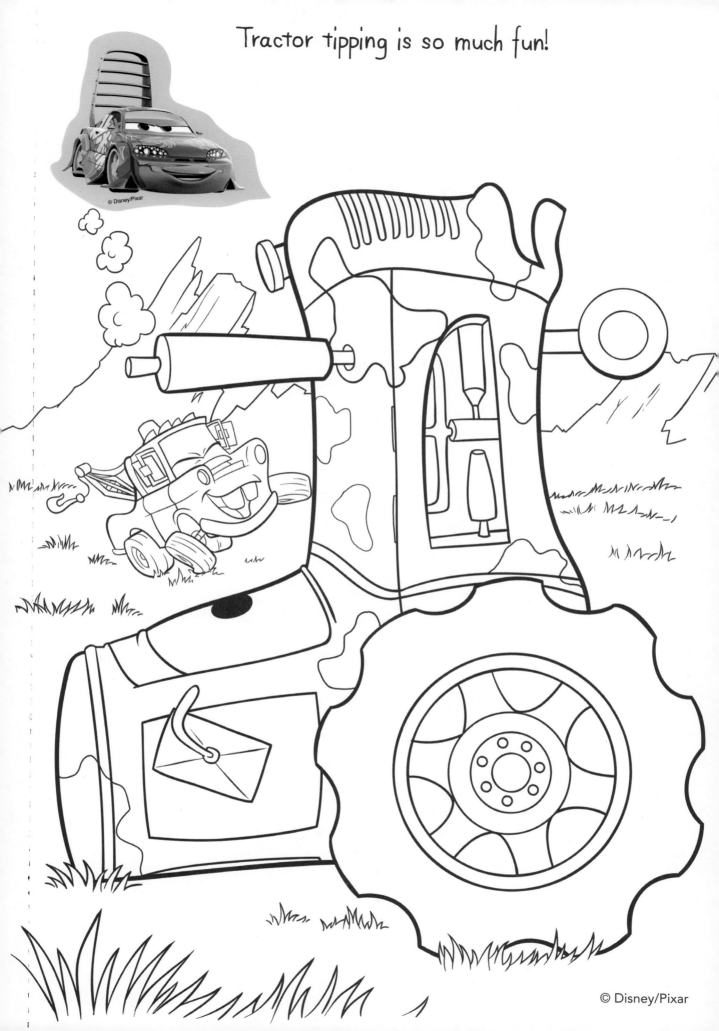

Sally loves living in beautiful Radiator Springs.

Fillmore brews tasty, organic fuel.

Lightning and his Radiator Springs pit crew make a great team!